For my dear and helpful daughters
Abigail, Jennifer, and Amanda
(and special thanks to
Ann D. and Amy E.)

Copyright © 1995 by Marylin Hafner
All rights reserved.
First edition 1995

Library of Congress Cataloging-in-Publication Data

Hafner, Marylin.
Mommies don't get sick / by Marylin Hafner.—1st ed.
Summary: While her mother is sick in bed, Abby tries to take care of her
younger brother and the house when her father has to go out for a while.
ISBN 1-56402-287-0
[1. Family life—Fiction. 2. Sick—Fiction.]   I. Title.
PZ7.H1198Mo   1995
[E]—dc20   94-24225

10 9 8 7 6 5 4 3 2 1

Printed in Hong Kong

The pictures in this book were done in watercolor and ink.

Candlewick Press
2067 Massachusetts Avenue
Cambridge, Massachusetts 02140

MOMMIES DON'T GET SICK!

Marylin Hafner

CANDLEWICK PRESS

CAMBRIDGE, MASSACHUSETTS

SATURDAY! NO SCHOOL! PANCAKES!

AND BACON!

Saturday was a special day at Abby's house. She didn't have to rush to school, and Daddy and Mommy were home from work.

But this Saturday when Abby woke up, something seemed different.

Abby went into Mommy's room.

Then she got dressed and went downstairs.

After breakfast, Daddy had to go to the store.

Abby started a load of laundry.

Sarah came to the door.

Abby managed to get the wet clothes into the dryer...but David was soaking wet and the floor was flooded.

She put David into dry overalls.

Dad heated Mom's special soup and Abby made ham sandwiches for lunch.

Then they all went upstairs to help Mommy get ready for lunch.